Karen's Movie Star

BABY-SITTERS
Little Sister

Karen's Movie Star
Ann M. Martin

Illustrations by Susan Crocca Tang

A
LITTLE APPLE
PAPERBACK

SCHOLASTIC INC.
New York Toronto London Auckland Sydney
Mexico City New Delhi Hong Kong

The author gratefully acknowledges
Gabrielle Charbonnet
for her help
with this book.

ISBN 0-590-50055-4

Copyright © 1998 by Ann M. Martin. Illustrations copyright © 1998 by Scholastic Inc. All rights reserved. Published by Scholastic Inc. The BABY-SITTERS LITTLE SISTER, LITTLE APPLE PAPERBACKS and logos are trademarks and/or registered trademarks of Scholastic Inc.

12 11 10 9 8 7 6 5 4 3 2 1   8 9/9 0 1 2 3/0

Printed in the U.S.A.   40
First Scholastic printing, October 1998

Dear Andrew

"Karen, hurry up!" called my stepsister, Kristy. "Nannie just made popcorn and hot chocolate!"

"Okay, coming!" I yelled back. On my way inside, I took one more running leap into the pile of leaves in our backyard. I landed with a satisfying *whump!* Then I dusted myself off and ran to the back door.

"Fall, fall, fall," I sang, hanging my jacket up in the mud room. "Fall, autumn, autumn, fall."

I hummed all the way into the big-house

kitchen. (I have a big house and a little house. I will explain why later.) In the kitchen, Kristy, my stepbrother David Michael, and Nannie were sitting at the table. A huge bowl of popcorn sat before them. A steaming mug of hot chocolate waited at my place.

"You seem chipper," said Nannie. (Nannie is my stepgrandmother.)

"I *am* chipper," I said, taking a handful of popcorn. Then I listed all the things I was chipper about.

"Number one, it is autumn. I love autumn," I said. "Crisp days, cozy evenings, hot chocolate. Number two, autumn means all the holidays are right around the corner: Thanksgiving, Christmas, New Year's. Number three, my little-house family will soon be home!" I finished happily.

"I know you are looking forward to that," said Kristy.

"Yes. In fact, I think I will send Andrew an e-mail right now. I will tell him that there are only seventeen days left until he comes

home." Andrew is my little brother. He is four. I am seven.

"Good idea," said Nannie. "When you are done, you can come back and help me set the table for dinner."

"Okeydokey," I replied, running to Daddy's office, where our computer was. Luckily no one else was using it just then. There are so many people at the big house that it is a miracle when a room is empty.

I turned on the computer and logged on to e-mail. Then I typed slowly:

Dear Andrew,

I am counting the days until you, Mommy, and Seth come home. There are seventeen days left. I cannot wait to see you again. It will be so great to sleep in my bed at the little house. It will also be kind of strange. I have been here at the big house for a long time.

Our new kitten, Pumpkin, is

growing fast. She is so funny and cute. She has not learned not to pounce on people yet. I am trying to teach her. Poor old Boo-Boo is not doing too well. But he has gotten very sweet. (If you can believe that.) I like Boo-Boo now. He even sleeps with me sometimes. I cannot wait for you to meet Pumpkin.

Oh! I almost forgot the most exciting news of all. Guess what. (You will never guess, so I will tell you.) A real, live Hollywood movie will be filmed here in Stoneybrook. And they are even using the outside of Daddy's house in the movie! They will be starting soon. I plan to be here a lot. I bet when the director sees me, he will realize that I could add a lot to the movie. I could play a Stoneybrook girl named Karen Brewer.

I have to go help Nannie set the

table now. I will send you another e-mail soon. I love and miss you very much.

Your big sister,
Karen

I clicked on the send button and sent my letter to Andrew. Although he is only four, he can read a lot of words. Mommy would help him if he got stuck. I love e-mail. I love to write letters. I love to get letters. With e-mail, I can send and receive letters much faster. In my opinion, the more things that can happen faster, the better. It is very, very hard for me to wait for anything. So you can imagine how hard it has been for me to wait for my little-house family to come home. It has been the hardest thing of my life.

I guess you are wondering who my little-house family is, and where they are. I will tell you — really fast.

I Will Be Home
for Christmas

A long time ago, when I was little, I lived here at the big house all the time. Back then my family was just me, Andrew, Mommy, and Daddy. Then Mommy and Daddy got divorced. Mommy took Andrew and me to live with her in a little house, not very far away. Daddy stayed in the big house, since he had grown up there. (We still saw him all the time. Both of my houses are in Stoneybrook, Connecticut.)

Mommy met a nice man named Seth Engle. They got married, and Seth became my stepfather. So my little-house family became me, Mommy, Andrew, and Seth. Also Seth's dog, Midgie, and his cat, Rocky.

Back at the big house, Daddy married Elizabeth Thomas. That made Elizabeth my stepmother. Elizabeth had been married before, and she had four children. They became my stepsister and stepbrothers. There is David Michael, who is seven, like me. Kristy is my favorite. She is thirteen. Sam and Charlie are very old. They are in high school.

Later Daddy and Elizabeth adopted my little sister, Emily Michelle. She is two and a half. She came from a faraway country called Vietnam. I love her very much.

We also have pets at the big house. Shannon is David Michael's humongous puppy. Scout is a Labrador puppy that Kristy is training to be a guide dog. Boo-Boo is Daddy's cat. He is very, very old. He used to be cranky and no fun. But lately he has gotten much nicer. He never scratches anyone anymore. He lets me pet him and brush him gently. And sometimes he even curls up on my bed with me. I like him much better now.

Our newest pet is an all-black kitten named Pumpkin. We got her around Halloween. She is gigundoly adorable. She is very playful and pouncy and climby and cute.

I also have a pet rat, Emily Jr. I named her after my little sister. Andrew has a pet hermit crab named Bob. And we both have goldfish. Mine is named Crystal Light the Second. Andrew's is named Goldfishie.

It is so busy and hectic and crazy at the big house that Elizabeth's mother, Nannie, came to live with us. She helps take care of everyone.

Usually my little brother, Andrew, and I spend one month at the little house with Mommy and Seth, and the next month at the big house with everyone else. But since last spring, Seth has had an important job in Chicago, which is very far away. So Mommy, Seth, and Andrew rented an apartment there. I went to Chicago with them at first, but I decided I missed my big-house family too much. So I came back. I have not lived at the little house for six whole months.

But now my little-house family was coming back for good! They would be home in time for Thanksgiving. Then I would leave the big house and spend a month at the little house. Then back to the big house again. Back and forth, back and forth. It is the story of Andrew's and my lives.

To tell you the truth, we are used to it. It is actually kind of fun. That is because we have two of lots of things, so we do not have to pack much when we switch back and forth. In fact, I made up special names for Andrew and me. I call us Andrew Two-Two and Karen Two-Two. We have two mommies, two daddies, two houses, two bedrooms (each), two bicycles, two sets of clothes. . . . The list goes on and on. I even wear two pairs of glasses. The blue ones are for reading, and the pink ones are for the rest of the time.

I was really looking forward to being with my little-house family again. But I was also glad I would have a few more weeks at the big house. I was very excited about the movie that would be filmed right in front of Daddy's house!

Not only that, but one of my favorite actors, Allison Hunter, was the star of the movie. Allison is eight years old. Ever since I heard about the movie, I have been planning ways to meet Allison. I want her autograph. I want to talk to her. Most of all, I want to ask her how I, Karen Brewer, can become a star too.

I bet when I meet Allison Hunter, we will become friends. When I am friends with Allison, maybe she will ask the director if I can be in her movie. Then I will be a star — at both of my houses.

Movie Excitement

The very next morning, before breakfast, the huge movie trucks arrived. They parked all up and down our street. Some were full of equipment, one was a minirestaurant for the movie workers, and some were for people to get dressed in. I wondered which one Allison would be in.

Before I left for school that day, I said good-bye to Boo-Boo and Pumpkin. "You two be good," I told them. "I will be home later this afternoon."

I am in second grade at Stoneybrook Academy. When I am at the big house, I take the bus to school with my best friend Hannie Papadakis, who lives across the street and one house down. At the little house, I take the bus with my best friend Nancy Dawes, who lives next door. Yes, that is right. I have two best friends. Hannie and Nancy and I call ourselves the Three Musketeers.

At school, Nancy was waiting for Hannie and me. She ran to us as soon as we got off the bus.

"Guess what!" she said. "My daddy saw in the newspaper this morning that the movie people need some extra kids for a crowd scene! We can audition for it!"

"Oh, my gosh!" I gasped. "That is wonderful!"

"We are all going to audition," said Sara Ford, who is also in our class. "The auditions will be in the Stoneybrook Middle School gym."

"When? When?" asked Ricky Torres. (He is my pretend husband.)

"Tomorrow," said Addie Sidney. She wheeled her wheelchair back and forth in excitement. "Tomorrow at two o'clock. I will be there."

Well. This was just about the most exciting thing that had happened all autumn.

"You know, if they hire us to be in the movie," I said, "we would be sure to meet Allison Hunter."

"Yes!" exclaimed Hannie eagerly.

"Ugh," said Omar Harris. "Why would you want to meet *her*? I hear she is stuck-up and unfriendly."

"I do not believe that," I said firmly. "She seems very nice in her movies. Anyway, I still want to meet her."

Then the bell rang, and it was time to go to class. Our teacher, Ms. Colman, is the best teacher ever. She is very patient and kind. All morning, I was thinking and thinking. The auditions would take place the next day. What should I do at my audition? Recite a speech or sing a song? I decided to ask Ms. Colman for help. Teachers always know about that kind of thing.

"Ms. Colman?" I said after everyone had left for lunch. (I asked Nancy and Hannie to save me a seat.)

"Yes, Karen? What is it? Are you all right? You were unusually quiet this morning."

"Oh, I am fine, thank you," I said. Then I told her about the auditions for *I'll Be Home for Christmas*. (That was the name of Allison Hunter's movie.) "Can you help me find a poem to audition with?"

"Certainly," said Ms. Colman.

"I was thinking of Shakespeare," I said. "He is always very popular."

"Hmm," said Ms. Colman. "Shakespeare is wonderful, but also sometimes difficult. How about if we find something else for you instead?"

"That would be okay," I agreed.

That night I could hardly sleep. I kept repeating my poem over and over to myself. I tried to put a lot of emotion into it.

When morning came, I was a nervous wreck.

The Audition

Early Saturday morning, the movie people began to get our house ready to be filmed. I helped by keeping all of our pets inside. The movie would use only the outside of the house. The producer told Daddy that all of the inside shots would be filmed at a studio in California. (I know it sounds weird. But that is how movies are made.)

The director, assistant director, and cameraman walked around our house many times, looking at it from all different directions. When I saw them from a window,

I waved. Sometimes they waved back.

For most of the morning I sat in a front window in the living room, watching the people outside. Boo-Boo sat next to me. I stroked his fur. He had lost some weight lately. He used to be gigundo, but now he is much thinner. Daddy says that is because he is getting old.

After lunch Elizabeth drove me to Stoneybrook Middle School for the auditions. All the way there, I kept repeating my poem to myself. This audition could make or break my movie career.

Tons of kids were at the school. I would have to put lots of emotion into my poem if I wanted to stand out.

"Hello, kids!" called a man. "Thank you for coming. As you know, we are holding auditions for walk-on parts in *I'll Be Home for Christmas.* Since these are non-speaking parts, called 'extras,' in a crowd scene, you do not have to give a speech. We just need to look at you."

"Oh, no!" I said to Hannie and Nancy. "I was up all night preparing."

"Me too," said Hannie. "I memorized a whole speech."

"I was going to sing a song," said Nancy. "But now I am glad I do not have to."

"Oh, look," I said, pointing. "That is the assistant director. I saw her this morning at my house."

Another assistant had started lining kids up in groups. Then two people would look at them and say whether they could stay or go. Most of the kids had to go. Only a few were right for the crowd scenes. I could not tell why some kids could stay and others not. I was excited to see that Addie Sidney and Sara Ford were both chosen.

We Three Musketeers waited for our turn. When the assistant director walked past us, I called, "Hello, Ms. Wynoski."

She turned to look at me, then she smiled. "Hello. You're the Brewer girl, aren't you?"

"Yes," I said eagerly. "I'm Karen Brewer.

These are my friends Hannie Papadakis and Nancy Dawes. We are here to audition for a part together. We are all best friends."

"Oh, good," said Ms. Wynoski.

"In fact," I continued quickly, "I have prepared a poem to recite. 'I think that I shall never see — ' "

"Just a moment, Karen," said Ms. Wynoski, holding up her hand. "These are non-speaking roles. Bill? Could you come here, please?"

I wanted to continue with my poem, but Ms. Wynoski was talking to one of the men who had been choosing kids. He looked at us and nodded, then walked away.

"Guess what?" said Ms. Wynoski. "I think you three best friends just got walk-on parts in the crowd scene."

Nancy gasped and put her hand to her mouth. Hannie and I beamed.

Ms. Wynoski gave us each a card. It said where to go and when to be there. Then she smiled at us and left to look at some other kids.

20

The Three Musketeers stood there, smiling. I was gigundoly happy that all of us had been chosen. As we waited for Mrs. Papadakis to pick us up, I had only one regret: I had not had a chance to perform my poem. How would my talent be discovered if I did not perform?

Karen Brewer:
Star-to-Be

Usually I love school. I am almost always happy to go to it. But I was not happy on Monday morning. Too many exciting things were happening at the big house. I did not want to miss anything.

"Yesterday they washed the whole outside of the house," I told Hannie and Nancy at lunchtime. "And they have been trimming bushes and raking leaves and washing windows."

"I guess they want your house to look

perfect for the movie," said Natalie Springer. (She is also in our class.)

I nodded. "They even planted a new tree in our front lawn! They told Daddy we could keep it after the filming."

"You are so, so lucky," said Natalie. Sara Ford nodded, and so did Addie.

I tried to look modest. "I know."

That afternoon after school, Hannie and Nancy came home with me. We could hardly see my house when we got off the school bus. There were huge trucks, humongous lights, and other pieces of equipment all over the place. It seemed as if a hundred people were swarming over our lawn. We did not see Allison Hunter anywhere.

"She was supposed to arrive today," I told Hannie and Nancy. "Maybe that lady knows where she is."

A tall, dark-haired woman was walking around slowly. She carried a large camera on her shoulder. She was looking through its eyepiece. I waited until she had glanced up, then said, "Ahem. Excuse me. Do you know where Allison Hunter is?"

"No, I am sorry," said the woman. "I do not see the stars too much. My name is Kathy Hopper. I am an assistant cameraman. Right now I am taking shots that will be edited into the final movie."

"Oh. That is very interesting," said Nancy. "But what about all this noise?" She waved her hand at the hubbub happening around my house. "Won't you record all the noise too?"

The woman shook her head. "No, I am not recording any sound right now. These are general shots of the house and neighborhood. They will probably be played with background music."

Ms. Hopper told us all sorts of interesting things about how a movie is made. For example, she said that every moviemaker films hundreds of scenes — sometimes the same scene over and over again. But only a

small number of them make it into the final version of a movie. That worried me. What if my crowd scene was edited out of the movie? I might never become a star.

Another thing Ms. Hopper told us is that the scenes in movies are not filmed in order. A scene at the very front of the movie might be filmed in the middle of the schedule, or even at the very end. Or they might film all of the outdoor shots one right after another, even though a lot of other stuff comes in between in the movie. It sounded very difficult and complicated. I did not know how they kept all this stuff straight.

Just before Hannie went home and Nancy's mother picked her up, Ms. Hopper told us an amazing thing. She said that the last couple of scenes to be filmed would take place in a snowstorm. But they could not be sure that it would snow here in Connecticut when they needed it to. So they were going to create tons of fake snow all over our house and yard.

I could not wait. Maybe the fake snow

would still be here when Andrew came home! I hoped so.

"Even though Hannie and Nancy and I do not have speaking roles," I told my big-house family at dinner that night, "we are thinking of ways to get ourselves noticed."

"I bet," muttered Sam, taking a bite of his chicken.

"Do not tell me," said Charlie. "Let me guess. You are all going to roll yourselves in glow-in-the-dark paint before you show up for your scene."

David Michael grinned.

"Boys," said Elizabeth in a warning tone.

They snickered.

I waved my fork at them. "You will be sorry you teased me when I become rich and famous."

Sam and Charlie and David Michael are not meanie-mos. They are usually very nice to me. But they do like to tease me sometimes.

"Um, Karen," said Kristy. "Please do not get your hopes up about becoming a star. It might not happen."

"It is good to think positively," I said.

"If I may change the subject for a moment," said Nannie, "I would like to discuss Boo-Boo. You all know he is getting older and more frail. Lately I have noticed that it is difficult for him to come downstairs for his meals."

"Hmm," said Daddy. "I have noticed that too. Poor old fella. What should we do?"

"I have an idea," said Nannie. "He spends most of his time upstairs anyway. We could fix him up a little spot in the upstairs hallway. Perhaps under that table in the hall. We could put his food and water there, and his kitty bed. Then he would not have to use the stairs at all."

"That is a good idea," said Kristy. "And we could move his litter box from the downstairs mud room to the hall bathroom."

"And we could put his toys right by his bed," I said. "We could even put a hot water bottle in his bed, to keep him cozy."

"Good," said Nannie. "Tonight I will do all of those things."

I finished eating my dinner quietly. Poor Boo-Boo. I decided to spend some extra time brushing him gently, after I had done my homework. I knew he liked that.

Allison Hunter!

On Tuesday afternoon I leaped off the school bus. (Hannie was not with me because she had a dentist appointment.) I could not believe she was at the dentist's while maybe Allison Hunter was in a trailer right in front of my house!

Nannie had a snack waiting. I wolfed down gingersnaps and a glass of milk. Then I ran to the living room window. (The movie people had asked us not to play outside, because they might be filming.)

I kneeled on the couch and peered outside. It was getting colder every day. I saw lots of people in heavy coats, but I did not see Allison. Maybe she was still in the makeup trailer. (All movie stars have to wear makeup. Even kids.)

Suddenly there was a small *pop*! I saw a flash of light, like a tiny bolt of lightning. Then all of the outside lights on the trailers and movie trucks went out.

Golly. What had happened? Was this part of the movie? I watched and waited, but the lights did not come back on. Five minutes later, our doorbell rang. I raced to the door, but Nannie beat me to it.

"Yes?" said Nannie.

"Hello, ma'am," said the man standing there. I recognized him. He was one of the film crew. "I am sorry to disturb you, but our generators have blown out. May I use your phone?"

"Oh, certainly," said Nannie.

I did not eavesdrop while the man was on the phone. (Eavesdropping is wrong.) I sat in the living room. Soon the man walked out of the kitchen.

"Is everything all right?" I asked him.

"Well, we have no electricity in our trailers," he told me. "So we have to stop filming for today." He turned to Nannie. "Good-bye, and thank you."

"Nannie, this is awful," I said after he left. "If they stop filming, Allison will leave."

"I have a thought," said Nannie. "Why don't you go across the street and ask Allison if she would like to come over for a cup of hot cocoa? If they have no electricity, then they have no heat. And it is cold out there."

"That is a great idea!" I said, already running for my coat.

I looked carefully both ways before I crossed the street. Then I saw the nice assistant director, Ms. Wynoski. She pointed out Allison Hunter's trailer for me.

I knocked on the door. My heart was beating so hard I could practically feel it through my coat.

A friendly-looking woman came to the door. "Yes?"

"Hello," I said. "My name is Karen Brewer. I live across the street, in the big house they are filming. I heard you do not have heat or electricity. Would Allison like to come over for a cup of hot cocoa?"

The woman smiled. "That is very kind of you. I am Belinda Hunter, Allison's mother. We are waiting for a car to take us to a hotel downtown, but I guess we can wait at your house. Thank you." She went inside the trailer for a moment. I could not see much. I was dying to know what a star's trailer looked like.

Soon Mrs. Hunter came back out again. She was followed by another woman with dark hair. "This is Sally Michaels," said Mrs. Hunter. "She is Allison's manager. And this is Allison."

I stared at Allison. She was eight years old, but she was hardly any taller than I am. She had long, straight brown hair and brown eyes. She did not smile.

At the big house, we sat in the living room while Nannie fixed cocoa. Usually only grown-ups are allowed to eat or drink in the living room. But today Nannie was making an exception.

"How do you like Stoneybrook?" I asked Allison.

"It is fine," she said, looking at her feet.

"Do you go to school?" I have always wanted to know this.

Allison looked at her mother, then at Sally Michaels. They both smiled at her. "I have tutors," said Allison. "I do not go to a regular school."

Hmm. Allison did not seem very happy or friendly. She was not exactly being mean, but she did not seem to want to talk. Still, I was the hostess here. She was my guest. I had to keep the conversation going.

"Where do you usually live?" I asked, passing her a plate of cookies.

She took a cookie. "Arizona."

I was surprised. I had expected her to say Hollywood, or maybe New York.

"What is it like in Arizona?" I said.

Allison perked up a little. "I love it there," she said. "The desert is very beautiful. My father and my little sister are there." Suddenly she looked sad. "I have not seen them in five weeks. It is hard to be away from my family. At least my mom can stay with me."

"But you are a big star," I said. "You get to meet other stars. People ask you for your autograph. You ride in limousines." I knew that I would love to be a star.

"It is not always fun," Allison said, sounding a little grumpy. "I do not have enough time to play. I miss my daddy and my sister and all my friends at my old school. Sometimes I have to get up very early."

I did not think I would mind all that, if I were a big star.

"Speaking of limousines," said Mrs. Hunter, "here is our car to take us downtown. Thank you very much for the cocoa and cookies, Karen and Mrs. Taylor." (Mrs. Taylor is Nannie.)

"Good-bye, Allison," I said. "I hope to see you again soon."

Allison gave me a little smile, and then they were gone. I sat on the living room couch and hugged myself. I had met Allison Hunter! A real, live star had sat right next to me and eaten our cookies. I wished I had asked her how I could become a star too, but I had not had enough time. I would ask her next time. (I just *knew* there would be a next time.)

Thanksgiving Plans

By Thursday, I had not spoken to Allison again. But both Hannie and Nancy had, while Nancy was at Hannie's house. (I had been helping Nannie make chocolates that day.) During recess at school we told one another everything Allison had said.

"I asked her how she got discovered," said Hannie.

"Good question! I wish I had thought of that," I said.

"She said she was shopping at a mall with her mother when she was just four years old," continued Hannie. "A talent agent spotted her. Soon she was doing television commercials. Then a director called her to be in a movie."

Hmm. That sounded awfully easy to me. Did it mean I had to start hanging out in malls more? Also, I am already seven. I should have been discovered three years ago.

"She has traveled all over the world," said Nancy.

"She has been to Disney World twelve times," added Hannie.

While we were talking, some of our classmates had gathered to listen. I felt very important, talking about Allison Hunter.

"With Allison right across the street," I said, trying to sound casual, "I will probably become good friends with her. Then maybe I can have a scene with her in her movie."

"The movie is already written," said Bobby Gianelli. Bobby is not as much of a bully as he used to be. But he still likes to rain on people's parades. "They will not rewrite it just so you can be in it."

I wanted to stick out my tongue at him. But I did not. I shrugged. "We will see," I said. That sounded very mysterious, I thought. "We will see."

On Friday night, Mommy called me from Chicago. We talk a lot on the phone. It helps us feel closer to each other.

"Mommy," I said. "I met Allison Hunter!"

"I want to hear all about it," said Mommy. "But first I have some good news for you. Andrew, Seth, and I will be coming back the day before Thanksgiving."

"Yay!" I cried, jumping up and down. Then I had a thought. "What about Thanksgiving dinner?" I asked. It is always a big deal at the big house. I had been looking forward to it.

"That is the good news," said Mommy. "Daddy and I talked, and we knew it would be difficult for you to leave the big house on a holiday. So we have decided that we

will all have dinner together on Thanksgiving — both of your families. Then you
can come home to the little house the next
day."

For a moment I could hardly speak. Both
of my families together? That does not happen very often.

"That is wonderful!" I shouted into the
phone. From the other room, Sam called,
"Indoor voice, Karen."

I used my indoor voice. "Oh, Mommy,
that is *excellent*. I will be so *thankful* to have
everyone here that I love."

"Me too," said Mommy.

Then I reminded Mommy that the Three
Musketeers had been chosen to be part of a
crowd in Allison Hunter's movie. "We will
be in one scene tomorrow and one scene
Sunday," I told her. "I am so excited, I cannot stand it."

"I do not blame you," said Mommy. "That
sounds like fun."

"Mommy?" I asked. "Will you travel the
world with me when I am a big star?"

Mommy laughed. "We will worry about that when it happens."

"Okay," I said.

That night I was too excited about filming the next day to go to sleep. Daddy read to me and tucked me in. I read to myself. Kristy came into my room and retucked me. I lay in bed singing quietly.

Daddy came in again. "Karen, it is getting late. Why aren't you asleep yet?"

"I am too excited," I told him. "Tomorrow might be the day I am discovered. I am also excited about Thanksgiving. I cannot sleep."

"I see," said Daddy. "Will it help if I tuck you in one more time?"

"Yes," I said. So Daddy kissed me and tucked me in one last time. Then he told me firmly to try to go to sleep.

I turned off the light. I flopped this way and that. But I could not stop picturing myself smiling for the cameras. I saw a director telling me she would make me a star. I saw myself signing autographs.

I tossed. I turned. I was wiiiiide awake.

Then I felt a soft thump on my bed. It was Boo-Boo. It is very hard for him to jump up nowadays, but he had climbed onto my bench and then onto my bed.

I reached for him and patted his head.

"Hello, Boo-Boo," I whispered. I scratched him behind his ears the way he likes. He purred and curled up next to me. His body was warm. His eyes were sleepy. Looking at his sleepy eyes made me feel sleepy too.

I snuggled up next to him and closed my eyes.

8

Three Extra Musketeers

On Saturday, as soon as it was light outside, I threw back the covers and leaped out of bed.

Downstairs Nannie was already making breakfast. Daddy had agreed to drive Hannie and me to Nancy's house. Then Mr. Dawes would drive us downtown, where we would report to the assistant director.

Hannie was waiting on her front porch when we came out of our house. She crossed the street carefully, then ran to our car. I looked at her clothes. We had each gotten a notice from the casting director saying what we should wear. We were supposed to wear casual play clothes, like jeans and a sweater or sweatshirt.

Hannie and I both smiled. We were wearing our nicest jeans. Under her coat, Hannie had on her special "I Love Greece" sweatshirt. (Her grandparents are from Greece. They sent her the sweatshirt.)

I was wearing my special yellow sweater that looks like a New York taxicab. It is very bright and colorful. I planned to leave my coat open a little bit, so the bright yellow would show.

"Okay, girls, hop in," said Daddy.

He dropped us off at Nancy's. I looked at the empty little house, right next door. In just a few days I would be living there again. It would feel very strange.

The three of us climbed into the Daweses' car. Nancy looked at us and grinned. She was wearing *brand-new* jeans. She unzipped her coat and showed us her dressiest sweater. Little fake pearls are sewn all over it. Hannie and I gave her high fives.

Downtown was very crowded. There were more cars than usual, and several of the big movie trucks were parked along one street. Ms. Wynoski was speaking through a megaphone.

She and another assistant director, Mr. Frazier, told us extras what would happen. Basically, Allison had to walk down a block in downtown Stoneybrook. She would look lost and upset. The rest of us would walk down the same block, some in the same direction as Allison, some in the other direction. None of us was supposed to look at Allison or react to her in any way.

That was it. Just walking and ignoring Allison.

"But that is not right," Hannie whispered to me. "If I were not in a movie, and I saw Allison walking down the sidewalk, of course I would turn and look at her. I might even ask for her autograph."

"I know," I whispered back. "But Allison

is not Allison in the movie. She is playing someone else. And that someone else is not famous. She is just a regular girl."

"Oh," said Hannie, nodding.

It is a good thing I know all about movies.

The two assistant directors divided up the extras. We Three Musketeers were told to walk in the same direction as Allison. We had to walk normally — no skipping or hopping. Allison would be walking slowly, so we would pass her. We were supposed to talk among ourselves, and pay no attention to Allison.

This is it, I told myself. It was not a very big part to play. But I had to start somewhere.

Three hours later I wondered if I really wanted to be a big star. We had been filming the same scene all morning. We had walked down the street seventeen times.

"I cannot believe how patient Allison is," said Nancy.

We were all leaning against a fire hydrant.

The assistant director had said we were done for the day. Because of our age, we could not work for very long. Mr. Dawes was waiting to take us home, but we wanted to make sure they did not need us any longer.

"Yes," I agreed tiredly. "She is a real professional."

It was true. Allison had walked up and down the street about a million times. She needed to look worried and upset for three hours. And she did it. She did not complain or drag her feet. She just did it, exactly the way the director said, again and again.

I guess that is why she is a big star.

If I were going to be a big star, I would have to act like that. To tell you the truth, I did not know if I was up to it.

We were only able to talk to Allison a couple of times. Hannie and Nancy and I had decided to compliment her a lot on her acting. That way she would know that we wanted to be friends. Then maybe she would help us get bigger roles in the movie.

But it did not work. Allison seemed uncomfortable when we complimented her. She did not want to talk about making movies or being a star. She was not mean, but she was not friendly.

Now it was time for us to go home. I knew I would see Allison again the next day, for a sledding scene that we were in. That would be my absolute last chance at stardom. Somehow I had to make sure Allison knew that I wanted to be friends with her.

"Excuse me, Allison," I said as she walked past us with her manager. She stopped and looked at me. "Would you like to come over for dinner tonight?" I had not asked Daddy, Elizabeth, or Nannie if this was okay. But I was pretty sure they would say yes. At the big house, one more mouth to feed does not make that much difference.

"Oh, um, thanks, but I do not think I can," said Allison. "I have to study my lines for tomorrow. And I have to go to sleep early."

"Oh," I said, disappointed. "That is too bad."

Allison looked as if she wanted to say something else. She stepped closer to me. "It is kind of hard for me to be friends with anyone," she told me softly. "Because I will be here only a short time. Then I will leave again. I am always coming and leaving. I never stay in one place too long."

"Oh," I said again. I did not know what else to say.

Allison gave me a little smile and walked away with her manager.

Karen's Last Chance

On Sunday afternoon, Nancy and I went to Hannie's house. Mrs. Papadakis was going to drive us to the big hill near the park, where our last scene would be filmed.

Once we were in the backseat, I motioned for my friends to lean closer. "Guys," I whispered, "I have been thinking."

"Uh-oh," said Hannie. Nancy giggled.

I frowned at them. "This is serious. Today is our last chance to be discovered. Today we have to show Allison and the director that we have what it takes to be movie stars."

"But we are just extras," said Nancy. "In yesterday's scene, we were in front of the camera for only about two seconds. Today we will be sledding down a hill. How can we show any talent?"

I held up a finger. "I have a plan," I said.

I could not help noticing that Hannie and Nancy suddenly looked worried.

So far this year, it had not snowed in Stoneybrook. But the movie crew's gigundoly huge snow-making machines had made tons of fake snow all over Sled Hill. It was just like the real thing. Tomorrow, those machines would throw snow all over our yard. It was very weird to see deep, cold snow piled high in one place, and then turn around and see everything else looking bare and brown.

For our scene today, we all had sleds. We went to the top of snow-covered Sled Hill and waited for instructions. I did not see Allison anywhere.

The assistant director Mr. Frazier trudged up the hill.

"Now, remember, kids," he said. "This scene is to show that Allison made new friends and had fun, even though she was lost. So we will be filming her sledding down the hill several times. At the end of the day, she will choose one person to sled down with her for a special scene."

I almost gasped. That person just had to be me!

"In the meantime," continued Mr. Frazier, "sled downhill normally, as if it were a typical snowy Sunday. Act natural."

"Humph!" I whispered to Hannie and Nancy. "Acting natural will not get us anywhere. Remember our secret plan."

"Okay," whispered Hannie. Nancy nodded.

Finally Allison showed up. She was wearing a purple ski outfit with fake-fur earmuffs. I looked down at my own clothes. Nancy and Hannie and I had worn the brightest clothes we could find.

The filming started. Sledding is fun, but today it seemed more like work. We would sled down the hill, then climb to the top and wait for the assistant director to signal us to sled down again. Sometimes we had to wait for a long time between rides so they could adjust the lights or the camera angles.

Nancy and Hannie and I tried to edge closer to Allison. She smiled at us once, but she was too busy concentrating on the director's instructions to talk.

We put my plan into action the very first time we sledded downhill. Mr. Frazier had told us to act natural, but what did that mean? We were kids, sledding.

So we had fun. Big fun. The three of us whooped and hollered and waved our arms and did fancy sledding tricks. We just *had* to be noticed! I sledded down the hill standing on one leg. I sledded backward. I sledded practically standing on my head. Hannie and Nancy did all the fancy moves they could think of.

But it did not work. The camera was pointing away from us, at the other side of the hill. We were not close enough to Allison. Even worse, no one from the movie told us that we had lots of talent.

By three-thirty it felt as if we had been sledding and waiting around for hours. The assistant director told us to take a hot-chocolate break. We did.

We stood next to the catering trailer, drinking our hot chocolate. I looked around for Allison. She had probably ducked back into the makeup trailer to have her face touched up. (I told you I know all about movies.)

"Hi," said a voice.

I looked around. It was Allison. She was smiling at us.

"You guys sure know how to do lots of tricks on your sleds," she said.

So she had noticed!

"It snows a lot here in the winter," I said. "We have lots of time to practice."

Allison laughed. "I had to take sledding lessons, just to film this scene. Where I live in Arizona, it hardly ever snows. And I have never been in another cold place long enough to learn how to sled. This is really fun."

Finally Allison wanted to be friends! I was about to answer her when the director called her. It was time for the last sled of the day. I was extra excited now. I was positive that Allison would choose me. After all, we were the only kids she had talked to all day.

At the top of the hill, Allison looked around. She put a mittened hand on her chin and thought. Then she pointed to some *boy* I didn't even know! He would be her special sled partner!

I felt like a pancake that a giant had stepped on. I could tell Hannie and Nancy felt that way too.

We watched glumly as Allison and the boy sledded down the hill together, laughing as they whizzed past. Then the director clapped his hands and yelled, "That is it for today, folks! Thank you very much!"

We trudged downhill slowly, too sad to sled. I was hoping to see Allison before we left with Mrs. Papadakis. I wanted to ask why she had not chosen me. But by the time we reached the bottom of the hill, Allison and her mother were being driven away in a big blue car. She had not even said good-bye.

I will not act that way when I am a star.

Fake Snow

Well, movie or no movie, Thanksgiving was coming, and I had a lot to do. On Monday at school we made Thanksgiving decorations for our classroom. First we each drew around our hands on a piece of orange construction paper. We cut out the hand shape. Then we glued colorful feathers to each of the four fingers. We drew a face on the thumb part, and there! It made a very nice turkey.

"Now, class," said Ms. Colman. "Please

take out a fresh sheet of paper. On the paper, write down three things that you are thankful for. In five minutes, we will read some of them aloud."

I love assignments like this.

Ms. Colman asked Ricky to read his first.

He stood up. "I am thankful that the Broncos are playing on Thanksgiving Day."

I could not help giggling. Boys are pretty silly sometimes.

"I am thankful my dog can catch a Frisbee in midair. I am thankful that my grandma and grandpa are coming to *our* house for Thanksgiving. Their house smells funny."

"Thank you, Ricky," said Ms. Colman. "Tammy?"

Tammy Barkan stood up. She is a twin. Her sister, Terri, sits next to her.

"I am thankful I have a twin sister," read Tammy. (Terri smiled.) "I am thankful that my parents are nice to me. I am thankful that my granny is recovering from her operation."

"Thank you, Tammy," said Ms. Colman.

I did not get to read my list out loud. (Rats.)

After school, I could hardly wait to get home. Today the movie crew would make fake snow all over our yard.

Hannie and I jumped off the school bus and ran to my house.

"Wow, look at that," said Hannie.

I was looking. A great big noisy machine was spraying heavy flakes of fake snow all over the front of our house. In some places, the snow was already six or eight inches deep. It frosted our windows and trees and bushes, just like real snow. There was even fake snow on the roof! Just ten feet away, in our neighbors' yard, were plain brown grass and trees with empty branches. Our yard was a winter wonderland.

"Cool," said Hannie. We grinned at each other. Then she went home to have a snack. I headed down our driveway and used the back door, so the snow would not have any footprints in it.

"Hi, Nannie," I called.

"Hi, sweetie," she said. "I have some hot cider and gingerbread cookies waiting for you."

"How do you like our special snow?" I asked, sliding onto a bench next to David Michael. (At the big house, there are so many people that we eat at one long table with two long benches.)

"It is awesome," said David Michael.

"It is very pretty," said Nannie with a smile. "Emily Michelle thinks so too, don't you, sweetie?"

"Snow!" said Emily Michelle.

After my snack I went upstairs. Kristy's room looks out over our front yard. (Mine looks out over the side yard. Kristy had given me permission to go into her room.) I sat on her hope chest in front of the window and watched the snow machines. They made a lot of noise.

"Meow," said a voice behind me.

I turned around to see Boo-Boo standing in the middle of Kristy's floor. He looked sleepy. I reached down and picked him up. He and I looked out the window together as the fake movie snow piled higher and higher.

After awhile I took Boo-Boo into my room and settled him on my bed. He looked chilly. I picked up a sweater off the floor and wrapped it around him.

Then I sat down at my desk to make Welcome Home cards for my little-house family. They would be here the day after tomorrow! Daddy had said I could go to the airport with him to pick them up. I was all quivery inside, like at Christmas. I would be so, so happy to see Mommy and Andrew and Seth again.

I was busily coloring in some pink hearts on Andrew's card when I felt a little paw swipe my leg. It was Pumpkin. I scooped her up and she patted my chin.

"I cannot play right now," I told her as I carried her to my bed. "But you snuggle up here and keep Boo-Boo warm, okay?"

I set her down next to Boo-Boo. Boo-Boo

opened one eye, then went back to sleep. Pumpkin curled up next to the old cat as close as she could, and she went to sleep too.

"Good girl," I said. Then I turned back to my cards.

Pre-Thanksgiving Plans

On Tuesday morning at breakfast, Nannie tapped her spoon against her juice glass.

"May I have your attention, please?" she asked. "Thanksgiving is just two days away. There are many things that need to be done. I expect all of you to pitch in and help."

"Okay," I said. "We do not have school tomorrow, so I can do a lot then."

"Thank you," said Nannie. "I will post a list on the fridge. You all sign up for what you feel like doing."

"All right," said Kristy, eating a spoonful of oatmeal.

"And Karen," said Nannie, "you should go through your room and decide if you need to move anything back to the little house."

I quit eating. Everyone at the table turned to look at me in surprise. None of us had thought much about my leaving.

"Okay, Nannie," I said.

Daddy gave me a special smile and patted my shoulder.

Before I left for school, I signed up for making place cards and helping to set the table.

At school we read Thanksgiving stories and made more decorations. Ms. Colman counted how many cans of food we had collected. We had been bringing in canned goods for weeks, collecting food for families who might not be able to have a Thanksgiving meal this year.

"Congratulations, class," said Ms. Colman. "You have collected seventy-three cans, and lots of other items besides. I am sure you will help many families have a good Thanksgiving."

We all cheered.

At recess the air felt colder. Hannie and Nancy and I swung a little bit to get warm, then sat on a bench to talk. I felt sad, but I did not know why.

"I am already hungry," said Nancy. "And we just ate lunch."

"It is because it is cold," said Hannie. "I am always hungrier when it is cold."

I did not say anything.

"I cannot wait for Thanksgiving," said Nancy. "Thanksgiving is my favorite meal of the whole year."

"One year we ate Thanksgiving dinner in a restaurant," said Hannie. "It was yucky. I like it much better at home."

I did not say anything.

"Karen, what is the matter?" asked Nancy. "You seem sad."

I did not know what to say.

"Come on, Karen," said Hannie. "You can

tell us. We are the Three Musketeers, re-member?"

That made me feel a little better. "I do not know why," I said, "but I feel very sad."

Hannie and Nancy looked at each other.

"You do not know why?" asked Hannie.

I shook my head. "I know I should feel happy. Thanksgiving is almost here. My little-house family is coming home. I might be in about two seconds of an Allison Hunter movie. . . ."

"Maybe it is not just one thing that is making you sad," said Nancy. "Maybe it is a bunch of little things. Think hard. Can you think of anything that has happened?"

I thought. Maybe Nancy was right. Maybe it was a bunch of little things, all adding up to sadness. "Maybe I am sad because Allison did not choose me to be her special sledding partner," I said. "And I thought that we would become friends, be-cause she is filming at my house. But it has not happened."

Hannie and Nancy nodded.

"And Boo-Boo is getting older all the time," I said. "I wish he were not so old and sick."

"Yeah," said Nancy.

"And I feel weird, leaving the big house in three days, to go back to the little house." As soon as I said it, I knew that was what was really making me sad. "I have been living at the big house for six months. I am used to it. I really, really, really miss Mommy and Andrew and Seth. And I am glad to be going back to the little house. But it will be weird too."

"I know," said Hannie. "It will be weird for everyone. I am used to having you right across the street. Now you will be gone sometimes."

Nancy smiled. "But I am happy, because you will be living next door to me again, every other month. I have missed not having you there."

I smiled back at her.

"You know, it will be different for awhile," said Hannie. "But then we will all be used to it again. And it will be okay."

"Yes," said Nancy. "You used to switch back and forth before, and it was okay. Now you will do it again."

"You are right," I said. I felt a lot better.

"It is not as if you are moving to Chicago," said Nancy. "That would have been awful. You will still be here in Stoneybrook. School will be the same. The Three Musketeers will be the same. And you will be with your mommy and Seth and Andrew again. It will all work out."

"Thank you," I said to Nancy and Hannie. "You have made me feel so much better." I gave them each a hug.

"What are Musketeers for?" asked Nancy.

Where's Boo-Boo?

That afternoon I raced home as soon as the school bus dropped me off. I was very glad to have Wednesday, Thursday, and Friday off from school. I love school, but sometimes it is nice to have a little vacation.

Today they were filming the big scene at our house. It was the most important part of the whole movie. Today Allison would trudge through the fake snow up our front walk. Then she would ring the doorbell. That was all that would be filmed. It was the end of the movie, when Allison finds her family again, after being lost.

Nannie had put a snack out for me in the kitchen. I ate it quickly. As I had hurried up our driveway toward the back door, I had heard the cameraman tell everyone to get ready to film in ten minutes. I did not have much time to get ready myself.

I wondered where Nannie was. I knew David Michael was at a friend's house. Daddy had gone to a meeting. Emily Michelle was probably napping but usually Nannie is in the kitchen waiting for me. I guessed she was upstairs. I did not have time to look for her.

As soon as I had finished my snack, I went into our mud room by the back door. That is where we keep our winter coats and boots. In the past few days, the weather had changed from autumnlike to winterlike. It was much colder outside. It almost felt as if real snow could fall.

I kicked off my sneakers and pulled out

my heavy winter boots. Then I found my down ski jacket and pants. I started to put them on. The movie people had asked Daddy to make sure none of us was looking out of the windows while they were filming, because our faces would show up in the movie. If we stayed away from the front windows, though, there was no way for us to watch Allison Hunter walk up our path and ring our doorbell.

But I had a plan. At the edge of our driveway was a big sycamore tree. It was not in the line of the cameras, so it would not show up in the movie. I did not think anyone would stop me from climbing it. My plan was to climb high in the sycamore tree and stay there during the filming. That way I would have the perfect view of Allison walking up our walk and ringing our doorbell.

I found my heavy mittens and stuck them in my pocket.

"Oh, there you are, Karen," said Nannie.

"I am glad you are home. What are you doing?"

"I am getting bundled up," I said. "It is cold out there."

"Yes, I know," said Nannie. "That is why I am so worried."

I stopped bundling. "Worried?"

"Yes. I am afraid Boo-Boo is missing," said Nannie.

"Missing? What do you mean?"

"I have been looking for him since after lunch," said Nannie. "He is not in his special box in the hallway. He has not eaten his food. I am worried. Maybe he got outside somehow. Or maybe he is trapped somewhere, like in a closet. Kristy and Sam have been looking for him since they got home from school."

Nannie looked very upset. I started peeling off my heavy clothes.

"Don't you worry," I said. "I will help look. I am small and can look in places that Kristy and Sam are too big for. I am sure Boo-Boo is around here somewhere."

"I hope you are right," said Nannie.

The big house really is a big house. There are nine bedrooms and a lot of bathrooms and all sorts of other rooms too. It is not easy to look for one cat who is lost in a gigundoly big house like that. But I tried my best.

I looked under everyone's beds. I looked in all our closets. I called and called him. I banged a spoon on a can of cat food. (That usually works.) Pumpkin came running to me again and again.

"Pumpkin, you are not lost. Please just ignore this can of cat food," I said. "And go find Boo-Boo. Tell him we are looking for him."

I could not find Boo-Boo anywhere. I started to feel worried myself. Maybe he *had* gotten out. I put on my coat and ran out the back door.

I called Boo-Boo very softly, so I would not interrupt the filming. They had been shooting the important scene all afternoon, and I had not seen one bit of it. But I did not care. Boo-Boo was much more important. I checked under bushes and in Daddy's greenhouse. I wished there were snow in the backyard, so I could see cat tracks. But there was nothing. I could not see a sign of Boo-Boo anywhere. Bullfrogs. Double bullfrogs.

As I walked along the driveway, a movie assistant came up to me.

"Is everything okay?" he asked.

I told him about Boo-Boo — that he was old and sick and now missing. I described what he looked like. The assistant was very nice. He said he would tell everyone to keep their eyes open for a cat that looked like Boo-Boo. There were many people around from the movie company. Maybe someone would see him.

"Thank you," I said. I went back inside. I was worried and upset, just like Nannie. Nannie and Kristy and Sam and I sat at the kitchen table, trying to think of places Boo-Boo could hide. We did not know what we would tell Daddy when he got home.

Karen's Great Idea

"Well," said Nannie finally. "We have looked everywhere. I think we will just have to wait for Boo-Boo to turn up. Maybe he is napping somewhere and did not hear us calling him. Maybe he is exploring a new place and does not want to come out right now. He will probably show up at dinner."

She did not look as if she really believed this.

Outside, the movie workers were taking down their huge lights. They were loading the equipment into their trucks. I had been waiting for this afternoon for weeks, and I had missed the whole thing. But I did not really care. Who wanted to see Allison filming a scene, anyway? She was not my friend.

The doorbell rang. I jumped up.

"Maybe it is one of the movie people!" I cried. "Maybe they found Boo-Boo!"

I ran to the front door and opened it. There stood Allison Hunter.

"Hello," she said. She seemed a little shy.

"Hello." I looked around. "Is this part of the movie? I thought you were finished."

"We are," said Allison. "Soon we will leave Stoneybrook. But I heard that your cat is missing. I came to help look."

Well. I forgave Allison for everything.

"Thank you," I said. "Come on in. We have looked everywhere. But we can look again. Maybe we need a new pair of eyes."

I introduced Allison to Kristy and Sam. I was proud that I could introduce a big star to my family, but I was even prouder that Allison wanted to help look for Boo-Boo.

The two of us looked in all the places I had looked in before, and even a few new places.

"I love your house," said Allison as we crawled under Daddy's bed. "It is so big, but it is also very cozy. It feels like a family lives here."

"Yes," I said, and then I sneezed because of all the dust bunnies under the bed. I told Allison about how Mommy and Daddy had gotten divorced, and then remarried, and about how now I had two families.

"And we are all going to eat dinner together on Thanksgiving," I finished. "It will be so great."

"It sounds great," said Allison. She crawled out from under the bed and sat back on her heels. "I would just like to see my one family for Thanksgiving. But I will not be able to. The very day after Thanksgiving, I have to be in New York to film some more scenes. So I cannot go to Arizona

to see my sister and my father. And they cannot come here. I really miss them."

Suddenly I realized something: Allison wished she had my life and my family just like I wished I were a star! I had thought her life must be wonderful. But it sounded as if most of the time she was busy and lonesome and homesick. I was sure she had fun too sometimes, but she was missing out on a lot of things that I had all the time. Hmm. Maybe being a big star was not as terrific as I thought.

Then I had a brilliant idea. I did not tell Allison my brilliant idea. Instead I walked her to the door, because she had to meet her mother. She and her mom would be staying in the hotel until late Thursday night.

I thanked Allison for helping to look for Boo-Boo. Then I ran to the kitchen. Elizabeth had just come home from work. Nannie was telling her about Boo-Boo.

"Nannie!" I said. "Elizabeth! Allison and her mom will be here till Thursday night. Allison is sad because she will not have

Thanksgiving with her family. Can they have dinner here with us on Thursday?"

Nannie and Elizabeth looked at each other.

"Sure, why not?" said Elizabeth. "We are already going to have so many people here that two more will not make much difference."

"Yea!" I cried, jumping up and down. It made the day seem less yucky. Now if we could just find Boo-Boo, everything would be great.

14

Daddy's Sad News

We did not find Boo-Boo all that evening. David Michael looked again as soon as he got home. Even Emily Michelle looked. But Boo-Boo did not come out for dinner. We could not hide how worried and sad we felt. That night, even Pumpkin seemed upset. She came into my room, meowing, and she poked around under my desk and up on my bed, as if looking for Boo-Boo. I did not sleep well that night.

When I woke up on Wednesday, I had a good thought and a bad thought:

1) My little-house family was coming home today!

2) Has Boo-Boo come back yet?

I jumped out of bed and threw on my jeans and a sweatshirt. Then I ran downstairs to the kitchen. Nannie was there, turning sausages in a frying pan. I could tell by her sad smile that Boo-Boo had not shown up yet.

I decided to look in every single square inch of our house after breakfast.

Elizabeth came in then, carrying Emily Michelle. "Good morning, everyone," she said. "Karen, are you excited about going to the airport later?"

"Yes, I really am," I said. "I cannot believe the day is finally here."

Elizabeth smiled at me and put Emily Michelle into her booster seat. Then Elizabeth leaned over and kissed my head. "We will certainly miss you during your little-house months. But I am happy you will be back soon."

"Thank you," I said.

"Juice! Juice!" said Emily Michelle, banging her hands on the table.

As Kristy was pouring out juice, Daddy came into the kitchen. He looked awful.

"Daddy, what is wrong?" I cried.

Daddy took a deep breath and sat down. "I am afraid I have some sad news," he said quietly. We all looked at him. Suddenly, I knew what he was going to say.

"I found Boo-Boo this morning," said Daddy. "He was in the very back of the linen closet in the hallway. He must have curled up there to take a nap yesterday. It looks as if he died in his sleep."

"Oh, no," said Elizabeth softly. "I am so sorry, honey."

"Boo-Boo is *dead*?" I asked. My voice cracked a little.

"Yes, sweetheart," said Daddy sadly. "He was a very old cat, and we knew he was sick."

I could feel hot tears welling up in my

eyes. I had known Boo-Boo my whole life. For most of my life, I had not liked him very much, because he had been grumpy. But lately he had become so nice. He had become my friend. I would miss him very much.

Everyone looked sad except for Emily Michelle, who did not understand what had happened.

"I am really sorry, Watson," said David Michael. "I know you had Boo-Boo for a long time."

"I got him as a little kitten," said Daddy, "years and years ago."

Elizabeth put her arms around Daddy. I got up from my seat and climbed on Daddy's lap. (I am not too old to do this, in emergencies.) He held me and I leaned against him. I was trying not to cry.

"Poor Boo-Boo," I whispered.

"We will tell your mother when we pick her up this afternoon at the airport," said

Daddy. "Boo-Boo was her cat too, for awhile."

I nodded.

For several minutes we all sat quietly in the kitchen together, feeling sad. That is what families do during hard times.

A New Friend

After breakfast, Daddy took Boo-Boo and put him in a beautiful wooden box that used to hold important papers in his office. We decided to bury Boo-Boo in our backyard the next day, when Mommy would be here too.

I went upstairs to my room. I did not feel like talking to anyone. Pumpkin came in and rubbed her little black head against my knee. I petted her softly and told her about Boo-Boo. She seemed to understand that something was wrong. She did not act playful, the way she usually does.

I sighed several times to myself, trying to let the bad feelings out. In a little while I would have to go downstairs and help Nannie get ready for our big Thanksgiving dinner. At least I could still look forward to that.

"Ohmygosh!" I suddenly said, sitting up. "I forgot to ask Allison and her mother to dinner tomorrow!"

I had to call her right away. But I did not know her number. I only knew the name of her hotel. I asked Elizabeth to help me get the number. But she had a better idea. First we found the number and called Allison to make sure she was there. Then we went to the hotel in person!

Mrs. Hunter opened the door to their room. "Hello, Karen," she said. "Nice to see you again."

"Thank you," I said. "I came over to ask Allison something."

A few days ago all I wanted to ask Allison was how to become a star, and whether she could get me a bigger part in her movie. That was when we were not friends. Now I wanted to ask her something much better.

"Hi, Karen," said Allison. "Come on in. Did you ever find Boo-Boo?"

Inside, the room looked like a small apartment. There was a tiny kitchen, a living area, and two bedrooms and a bathroom. You might think, since a star was staying there, that it would be totally fancy inside. But it looked very normal. There were no fake tiger-skin rugs on the floor. No gold curtains. No fancy furniture. It just looked like a regular, comfortable hotel room. I liked it.

I sat down and answered Allison's question. I told her how Daddy had found Boo-Boo this morning, and how we would bury him tomorrow. Allison was very sad to hear about it.

"I have a cat of my own at home," she said. "I know how upset I would feel if anything happened to her. I am sorry, Karen."

"Thank you," I said. "But actually, that is not why I came over. I came over because no one should be by themselves on Thanksgiving. Daddy and Elizabeth said I could ask you and your mom to come to our house tomorrow for dinner. There will be about a million of us. But it will be very fun. And maybe if you are surrounded by all of my families, you will not miss your own family so much."

Allison's face lit up. "I would love to! Mom, can we, please?" She turned back to me. "We were going to have Thanksgiving dinner here. But I would much rather come to your house."

"Are you sure it is okay?" asked Mrs. Hunter.

I nodded. "Yes. We will be eating at two o'clock."

"Great!" said Allison. "Thank you so much."

I was glad that I had made Allison happy.

We sat and talked for awhile longer. Allison was excited because, in two weeks, she would finish filming the movie, and she could go home and see the rest of her family. But she could stay with them for only a month before she had to head off again to make another movie.

It is much harder being a star than you would think.

Allison told me that the reason she had not picked me for the special sledding scene on Sunday was that the producers had wanted her to pick a boy. I felt much better when I heard that. Allison was becoming a friend, and I was very lucky. On the way home, I thought about how much I had to be thankful for, even though Boo-Boo was gone.

Welcome Home, Andrew!

Daddy and I were supposed to pick up my little-house family after lunch. But when he called the airport to check on the flight, they gave him bad news.

"There was a huge snowstorm in Chicago last night," he told me. "More than a foot of snow has fallen. Mommy's plane cannot leave. They do not know when it will be able to leave."

"What?" I cried. "I have been waiting for them to come for so long! It is Thanksgiving! I told Allison that both of my families would be here. And we need to tell Mommy about Boo-Boo! They cannot be late. I cannot wait any longer!" Before I knew what was happening, I had burst into tears.

Daddy kneeled down and put his arms around me. I took off my glasses and buried my face in his shoulder. (It is hard to cry when you wear glasses. They get all fogged up from the tears.) I do not know how long I cried. It felt like a long time. Finally I was all cried out. Daddy handed me a tissue. I wiped my nose.

"I am sorry, Karen," Daddy said softly. "I think I know how you feel. Sometimes it is all too much."

I nodded and hiccuped.

"But this does not mean that Mommy will not be coming home at all," continued Daddy. "It just means she will be a bit late. As soon as the snow stops and they plow the runways, her plane can leave. There is a very good chance that we will all have Thanksgiving together tomorrow. Okay?"

I nodded again. I felt very tired.

Nannie knelt beside me. "I know you are upset, Karen," she said. "But I could really use your help. We need to get everything ready for tomorrow. If your mother does come, it is important that we have a good meal ready for her, right?"

"Right," I whispered.

For the rest of the afternoon I was Nannie's special helper. I put up Thanksgiving decorations. I helped set the gigundo dining room table that we hardly ever use. I dusted extra chairs. I made beautiful place cards to show everyone where to sit. Three of the cards were for Mommy, Seth, and Andrew.

After dinner David Michael, Kristy, Emily Michelle, and I watched a movie. Kristy made popcorn. The house was already full of wonderful cooking smells. It smelled like Thanksgiving. But it did not feel like Thanksgiving.

Every so often, Daddy would call the airport. By the time I had to go to bed, Mommy's plane had not taken off yet. I could not believe it.

Kristy helped me get ready for bed. I had gotten used to having Boo-Boo sleep with me. The night before Pumpkin had slept with me instead. Kristy found her and put her on my bedspread. I petted her while Kristy tucked me in.

"Kristy, what if Mommy does not get here in time?" I asked. "I wanted to have both my families together for Thanksgiving. I promised Allison everyone would be here."

Kristy patted my hand. "Try to think positively," she said. "You never know what will happen."

I did not think I would ever be able to go to sleep. But I was worn-out and tired. The next thing I knew, a dim gray light was coming through my window. I sat up and opened my curtain. For a moment I thought the movie people had sprayed fake snow all over our side yard too. Then I realized what had happened: The same storm that had hit Chicago had finally made its way to Stoney-brook, Connecticut. There was about a foot of snow on the ground. It looked beautiful.

Suddenly my bedroom door burst open.

"Karen!" shouted Andrew.

"Andrew!" I screamed. I flung myself out of bed and grabbed him in a huge bear hug. "You made it!" I said. "You really made it!"

"Hi, honey," said Mommy. She and Seth came in my room.

"Mommy!" I yelled. "Seth!"

We all hugged and kissed and hugged again. I was so, so, so, so happy. They told me they had finally gotten home around five o'clock in the morning. But they could not wait to see me. They had eaten breakfast and hurried over to the big house.

I told them everything about the movie, and about Allison coming for dinner. Then I told Mommy about poor Boo-Boo.

"Oh, dear," she said, looking sad. "I knew he was getting old. But I sort of thought he would last forever."

Andrew and I decided to write a farewell poem to Boo-Boo. We were going to hold the funeral at one o'clock, before Allison arrived. But first Andrew had to take a nap.

I smiled as Mommy and Seth went downstairs for a cup of coffee. My family had come home, in spite of the snowstorm. It was just like Allison's movie, *I'll Be Home for Christmas*. I was very thankful.

Farewell to Boo-Boo

Because of all the real snow in the backyard, Daddy, Seth, Sam, and Charlie had to clear a space and then dig a deep hole.

We bundled up and gathered around the grave. I felt sad all over again. I had been so happy, then so sad, all in one day. It was exhausting.

"Today we have gathered to say good-bye to an old friend," said Daddy quietly. That was all it took. I started crying. Mommy started crying. Nannie sniffled. Elizabeth and Kristy blinked back tears. Even Sam and Charlie looked sad. David Michael's and Andrew's lips quivered. (Thank heavens Emily Michelle was inside taking her nap. The nursery monitor was clipped to Nannie's belt.)

"Boo-Boo was not always the most affectionate cat," continued Daddy. "But he was ours for a long time, and he was my friend. I will miss him. I am glad he died at home, with us, his people, and that his end was peaceful."

I held tightly to Mommy's hand.

"Karen?" asked Daddy.

I stepped forward to read the poem Andrew and I had written. "It is called 'Dear Boo-Boo,' " I began. Then I read:

We miss you, dear Boo-Boo,
We miss you so much,
Although until recently
You didn't like us to touch
You.

But lately you had been
So nice and so sweet.
When you curled up with us,
We thought it was neat.

And now you are gone
Forever, they say.
Dear Boo-Boo, sweet Boo-Boo,
We wish you could stay.

Mommy blew her nose. Then Daddy gently placed Boo-Boo's box in the deep hole. Andrew and I put our poem on top. Sam and Charlie filled the hole in with dirt. Then Seth hammered in a small wooden cross that he had quickly made. (Seth is an excellent carpenter.) A cat face was carved on it, and Boo-Boo's name, and the years that he was alive. Daddy thanked him.

Then we all spread fresh, soft, white snow over everything, to make it look pretty again.

Boo-Boo's funeral was over. I held

Mommy's hand and Andrew's hand. We stood quietly for a few moments.

Then it was time to go inside, warm up, and get ready for Thanksgiving. Allison would be here soon! Maybe she would cheer me up.

Happy Thanksgiving!

Allison and her mother arrived right on time. I had changed into a corduroy party dress, with white tights and shiny black shoes. Allison had dressed up too, but she was not wearing a movie-star dress. It was not gold or silver. It did not have fake fur or jewels sewn on it. She looked normal.

"Hi!" I said. "Thanks for coming."

Mrs. Hunter had brought a cake for dessert. Nannie thanked her and led her into the kitchen.

"How did the funeral go?" asked Allison.

"It was awful," I said. "But it was good too."

"I know," said Allison. "I can imagine it. Do you feel too sad to play?"

"No," I said. "Playing is just what I need."

The big house had never been so hectic or so noisy. It was great. I introduced Allison and her mom to Mommy, Seth, and Andrew. Then Kristy, David Michael, Allison, Andrew, Emily Michelle, and I played hide-and-seek downstairs. (Emily Michelle is not very good at hiding. And she always gives herself away. But we helped her.)

Soon the smells of the delicious food were too much to bear. Mommy, Elizabeth, Nannie, Seth, and Daddy started bringing bowls and plates and trays and platters out of the kitchen and into the dining room. In the dining room were the big table for grown-ups and teenagers and a smaller table for us younger kids. On our table was a gigundoly fancy tablecloth, and fancy napkins, and good china and everything. It looked beautiful.

Allison and I took our plates and lined up to be served.

"This is so wonderful," said Allison, looking at all the food. "Last year for Thanksgiving my sister and daddy flew to London to be with me and Mom. Room service in our hotel sent up a meal, but it was not the same. They did not have real Thanksgiving food. This is much better."

I smiled at her. A big star thought my family was special. I sometimes wanted to be a big star, and Allison Hunter, a big star, sometimes wanted to be *me*. It was very satisfying.

We all ate a lot, because that is what you do on Thanksgiving. When I looked at the grown-ups' table, everyone was smiling and talking nicely together. Daddy and Elizabeth and Mommy and Seth do not always enjoy being together. But today everyone was happy.

After we finished firsts, we had seconds, and then even thirds. Then we all decided to lie around in the family room until we could face dessert. After awhile, Allison sat up and said, "Oh! I almost forgot. I have a surprise for you."

Allison's Surprise

Well. There is nothing I like better than a good surprise.

"What? What is it?" I asked.

Allison went into the hall and took a small package out of her backpack. It was a videotape.

"This is a very, very rough edit of what we have filmed so far on *I'll Be Home for Christmas*," she said. "It is not at all what the final movie will look like. But I thought you would like to see the scenes that you were in."

"Oh, my gosh!" I said. "We will be the first people to see it! Thank you, Allison!" This was so great. Months from now, people would line up to see the new Allison Hunter movie. And I would already have seen it. I wished Hannie and Nancy could see it too.

The tape was not as long as a real movie, only about forty minutes. But we saw some scenes that showed Allison getting lost, and we saw her family looking for her. It was very funny, but sometimes it was sad too, for instance, when Allison realized she was lost, and she started crying, all alone, on a park bench.

Her tears looked totally real. I felt sorry for her.

"You are a very good actress," I whispered to her. This time she grinned at me.

Then we saw some of the Stoneybrook shots.

"Look! There is Karen!" cried Kristy.

It was the shopping scene downtown. People walked past Allison, not paying attention to her. Allison looked lost and sad. Then I saw the Three Musketeers. We walked past Allison, laughing and talking. To tell you the truth, we stuck out. We did not blend into the scene like the other people did.

Then there was a scene of Allison in a train station, trying to make a phone call. She did not have enough change. She cried again.

Then we saw the sledding scene. The camera focused mostly on Allison. In the background, I could see Hannie, Nancy, and me performing tricks on our sleds. Once again, we stuck out. I hated to think it, but we looked silly. My plan had backfired. I was sure that these scenes would be edited out of the movie. I was kind of relieved. I realized I did not really want millions of people to see me acting that way.

"Hams R Us," Charlie said with a snicker.

"Okay, Charlie, enough," said Elizabeth.

The very last scene was the big one with all the fake snow, shot on the day that we first missed Boo-Boo. Allison walked up to our doorway and rang the bell. We saw her do this from many different angles, over and over.

"Sorry," said Allison. "They did not edit this part down yet."

"Hey, look!" said Andrew. "Look in the upstairs window!"

In this shot, we saw the whole front of our house. We all looked at the row of upstairs windows, where Andrew was pointing. And there, sitting in one of the windows, was Boo-Boo. He was looking out at the yard.

"That is the day we were looking for him," I said. "If he was sitting in a window, how come we did not see him?"

"Maybe he just sat there for a minute, then went in the back of the closet," suggested Kristy.

The TV screen went blank. The tape was over.

"It was very nice to see Boo-Boo one last time," said Daddy. "Thank you, Allison."

"Yes, thank you," I said. "The movie looks like it will be great. And everyone can see Boo-Boo again."

"Yes," said Allison, smiling.

Allison and her mom stayed with us through the evening, when we had leftover turkey sandwiches and more dessert. It was wonderful. When they left, Allison promised to write to me, and I promised to write back. I was glad to have a new friend.

Later, Mommy, Seth, and Andrew left also. In the morning I would pack up anything I needed and move to the little house for awhile.

Life was back to normal.

I Am Thankful For . . .

"Is this everything?" asked Kristy the next morning.

I looked around my room at the big house.

"Yes, I think so," I said. "I need to take this cardboard box and this suitcase. Everything else can stay here until I come back."

Kristy leaned down and hugged me. "I will see you very soon," she said. "Because I am going to baby-sit for you and Andrew next Wednesday night."

Kristy and her friends have a baby-sitting business. I love having Kristy baby-sit for us.

Kristy left to tell Daddy I was ready. I sat on my bed and looked around one last time. This was the longest I had been at the big house since Mommy and Daddy had gotten divorced. It had been fun, even though I had missed Mommy, Andrew, and Seth so much. But I was happy to be going back to the little house. I had missed my little-house room and my little-house stuff. Also, sometimes it is peaceful and restful at the little house. It is never peaceful or restful at the big house. But it *is* always exciting and noisy and fun.

Pumpkin leaped up onto my bed then.

" 'Bye, Pumpkin," I said, trying to sound cheerful. "I will miss you, but I will see you soon. I always come back."

I thought about the list of things I am thankful for, the list Ms. Colman had asked us to write. I had not been able to read my list out loud. And on Thanksgiving Day, there had been so many people and so much commotion that we had not shared our thanks with one another.

I decided to make a new list. I sat at my desk and took out a sheet of paper. Then I carefully wrote:

THINGS I AM THANKFUL FOR
BY KAREN BREWER

1) I AM THANKFUL THAT I HAVE TWO PARENTS WHO LOVE ME, AND TWO STEPPARENTS WHO LOVE ME.
2) I AM THANKFUL THAT BOO-BOO AND I BECAME FRIENDS BEFORE HE DIED.
3) I AM THANKFUL THAT MOMMY, ANDREW, AND SETH ARE HOME NOW.
4) I AM THANKFUL FOR ALL MY FRIENDS: OLD FRIENDS LIKE HANNIE AND NANCY, AND NEW FRIENDS LIKE ALLISON.
5) I AM THANKFUL FOR MS. COLMAN.
6) I AM THANKFUL FOR PUMPKIN.

7) I AM THANKFUL I AM ME, AND NOT A FA-
MOUS MOVIE STAR. (YET.)
8) I AM THANKFUL ...

I kept writing until Daddy called me to go
to Mommy's house. The list went on and on.

L. GODWIN

About the Author

ANN M. MARTIN lives in New York City and loves animals, especially cats. She has two cats of her own, Gussie and Woody.

Other books by Ann M. Martin that you might enjoy are *Stage Fright*; *Me and Katie (the Pest)*; and the books in *The Baby-sitters Club* series.

Ann likes ice cream and *I Love Lucy*. And she has her own little sister, whose name is Jane.

Little Sister

Don't miss #104

KAREN'S CHRISTMAS CAROL

"Karen, how about you? How was your day?" asked Seth.

"It was excellent," I replied. "The community center is putting on *A Christmas Carol*. They need kids to be in it. I am going to audition!"

Suddenly Andrew spoke up.

"We do dishen at school," he said. "One and one is two!"

At first I did not know what Andrew was talking about. Then I figured it out.

"I did not say addition, Andrew. I said *audition*. That means to try out. I am going to try out to be in the play," I said.

"Oh. Can I be in the play too?" he asked.

I looked at Andrew. Sometimes he surprised me. I did not think my little brother would want to be in a play. Especially if it meant being away from Mommy.

Little Sister

by Ann M. Martin
author of The Baby-sitters Club®

More Titles... ➡

The Baby-sitters Little Sister titles continued...

❑	MQ26301-3	#73	Karen's Dinosaur	$2.95
❑	MQ26214-9	#74	Karen's Softball Mystery	$2.95
❑	MQ69183-X	#75	Karen's County Fair	$2.95
❑	MQ69184-8	#76	Karen's Magic Garden	$2.95
❑	MQ69185-6	#77	Karen's School Surprise	$2.99
❑	MQ69186-4	#78	Karen's Half Birthday	$2.99
❑	MQ69187-2	#79	Karen's Big Fight	$2.99
❑	MQ69188-0	#80	Karen's Christmas Tree	$2.99
❑	MQ69189-9	#81	Karen's Accident	$2.99
❑	MQ69190-2	#82	Karen's Secret Valentine	$3.50
❑	MQ69191-0	#83	Karen's Bunny	$3.50
❑	MQ69192-9	#84	Karen's Big Job	$3.50
❑	MQ69193-7	#85	Karen's Treasure	$3.50
❑	MQ69194-5	#86	Karen's Telephone Trouble	$3.50
❑	MQ06585-8	#87	Karen's Pony Camp	$3.50
❑	MQ06586-6	#88	Karen's Puppet Show	$3.50
❑	MQ06587-4	#89	Karen's Unicorn	$3.50
❑	MQ06588-2	#90	Karen's Haunted House	$3.50
❑	MQ06589-0	#91	Karen's Pilgrim	$3.50
❑	MQ06590-4	#92	Karen's Sleigh Ride	$3.50
❑	MQ06591-2	#93	Karen's Cooking Contest	$3.50
❑	MQ06592-0	#94	Karen's Snow Princess	$3.50
❑	MQ06593-9	#95	Karen's Promise	$3.50
❑	MQ06594-7	#96	Karen's Big Move	$3.50
❑	MQ06595-5	#97	Karen's Paper Route	$3.50
❑	MQ06596-3	#98	Karen's Fishing Trip	$3.50
❑	MQ49760-X	#99	Karen's Big City Mystery	$3.50
❑	MQ50051-1	#100	Karen's Book	$3.50
❑	MQ50053-8	#101	Karen's Chain Letter	$3.50
❑	MQ50054-6	#102	Karen's Black Cat	$3.50
❑	MQ43647-3		Karen's Wish Super Special #1	$3.25
❑	MQ44834-X		Karen's Plane Trip Super Special #2	$3.25
❑	MQ44827-7		Karen's Mystery Super Special #3	$3.25
❑	MQ45644-X		Karen, Hannie, and Nancy The Three Musketeers Super Special #4	$2.95
❑	MQ45649-0		Karen's Baby Super Special #5	$3.50
❑	MQ46911-8		Karen's Campout Super Special #6	$3.25
❑	MQ55407-7		BSLS Jump Rope Pack	$5.99
❑	MQ73914-X		BSLS Playground Games Pack	$5.99
❑	MQ89735-7		BSLS Photo Scrapbook Book and Camera Pack	$9.99
❑	MQ47677-7		BSLS School Scrapbook	$2.95
❑	MQ13801-4		Baby-sitters Little Sister Laugh Pack	$6.99
❑	MQ26497-2		Karen's Summer Fill-In Book	$2.95

Available wherever you buy books, or use this order form.

Scholastic Inc., P.O. Box 7502, Jefferson City, MO 65102

Please send me the books I have checked above. I am enclosing $_____
(please add $2.00 to cover shipping and handling). Send check or money order – no
cash or C.O.Ds please.

Name_____Birthdate_____

Address_____

City_____State/Zip_____

Please allow four to six weeks for delivery. Offer good in U.S.A. only. Sorry, mail orders are not avail-
able to residents of Canada. Prices subject to change.   BSLS398